THE GUILD OF LIGHT

THE GUILD OF LIGHT

Re-Genesis

JEFF MALDEREZ

A. NOBODY

&

SELF

Jeff Malderez Artist

Contents

Prologue   4

Part One   9
  1 The Dance of Infinity   11
  2 Beyond the Game   17
  3 Re-Genesis Revealed   23

Part Two   29
  4 Witnessing the Other   31
  5 The Beauty of Flaws   39
  6 The Search for Sacred Purpose   45

Part Three   53
  7 The Cosmic Mirror   55
  8 The Awakening   61
  9 You Are the Other   69

Part Four   77
  10 Beginning Again   79
  11 The Seed of Light   85
  12 The Eternal Return   91

Epilogue   97

bio.site/jeffmalderez

Elements of AI used, including outline, structure and edits.

Released under Creative Commons Attribution-Noncommercial 4.0 International License.
Https://creativecommons.org/licenses/by-nc/4.0/

You are free: to share – to copy, distribute, display, and perform the work; to remix – to make derivative works.

Under the following conditions: attribution – you must attribute the work in the manner specified by the author or licensor (but not in any way that suggests that they endorse you or your use of the work); noncommercial – you may not use this work for commercial purposes. Any of the above conditions can be waived if you get permission from the copyright holder directly.

First Published 2025. Jeff Malderez, A. Nobody & Self, IngramSpark.

Paperback ISBN: 979-8-9918841-5-0
Hardback ISBN: 979-8-9918841-6-7
Ebook ISBN: 979-8-9918841-7-4

Some rights reserved © Jeff Malderez, 2025.

FOR YOU...

...yes, I mean YOU!

...I was wondering when you would read this...

...your timing is DIVINE!

Prologue

A Game Before Creation

Aria floated in a space that wasn't really space, wrapped in a timeless light that held no weight or form. It was neither warm nor cold, neither dark nor bright. It simply *was*. She was there, yet she wasn't alone. Across from her sat her Self—or maybe God—or maybe something else entirely. The being took the form of... well, whatever it wanted, and today it had chosen a slightly ridiculous version of Aria herself, but with an enormous grin and oversized glasses.

They sat together, suspended in a vast nothingness, playing a cosmic game of tic-tac-toe.

"You're not going to win," her Self said with a playful smirk, drawing an X in the bottom left corner of the grid that hung in the air between them.

Aria rolled her eyes, drawing an O in the center. "I'm not trying to win," she replied. "Isn't that the point of this whole exercise?"

Her Self laughed, a sound that echoed with the wisdom of eons and the carefree nature of a child. "You've learned something, I see. But tell me, isn't it odd that you're playing a game that can never be won?"

"That's life, isn't it?" Aria shrugged, crossing her arms. "Besides, I don't mind a draw. It's better than constantly fighting to win."

Her Self placed another X on the board, chuckling as it leaned back, watching her. "True. It's funny, isn't it? You're about to go back into that world where everyone thinks it's about winning. That it's about having the last move, the last word, the last breath."

"And you're here," Aria said, "to remind me that it's not."

The being nodded. "And what is it really about, Aria?"

She paused, her hand hovering over the grid. She wasn't sure why she always hesitated before answering questions like these. It wasn't like she didn't know the answer. After all, she had been in this space, with this being—this higher Self—countless times before. But each time she sat at the edge of her own existence, preparing for a new incarnation, the answer always felt just out of reach.

"It's about love," she finally said, tracing her O onto the board. "And growth. And the cycles that never end."

"Ah," her Self grinned wide, clapping with exaggerated enthusiasm, "very good! Love and growth. And cycles. You're catching on."

Aria couldn't help but smile at the being's antics. "I'm catching on, but I'm also going back," she said. "I'm going back to start all over again."

"Back to Earth," her Self said with a knowing tilt of its head. "A place where you will forget, once again, that you already know all of this. Funny, isn't it?"

"Funny isn't the word I'd use," Aria muttered. She looked down at the floating tic-tac-toe board. It was almost full now, and she could already see the stalemate forming. It was, as always, a draw.

"You're about to step into the chaos again," her Self said softly, the playful tone gone now, replaced with a seriousness that came from the depths of eternity. "The world below is struggling. They've forgotten the essence of it all—forgotten themselves."

"I know," Aria said quietly. "But that's why I'm going back. They need a reminder."

Her Self leaned closer, eyes sparkling behind the oversized glasses. "Do you remember why you chose this path in the first place?"

Aria nodded. "To help them remember. To help them find their way back to love."

Her Self smiled. "And you will. But it won't be easy. You know that, don't you?"

"Nothing worth doing ever is," Aria replied, feeling the familiar heaviness settle in her chest. "But it's not just them. I have lessons to learn too."

"Ah, the eternal student," her Self teased. "You always were a glutton for growth."

Aria laughed. "Well, I've lived as almost everything now—human, animal, elements, even galaxies. And yet... there's always something more."

Her Self reached out, gently tapping her forehead. "That's because *infinity* is a rather long time to spend learning. And you've chosen one of the most complicated lessons of all: being human."

"Humans," Aria sighed, shaking her head. "The ones who've forgotten who they really are."

Her Self nodded slowly. "They've forgotten, yes. But they're waking up. You'll be part of that—part of the great re-awakening, the Re-Genesis."

"The Re-Genesis," Aria repeated, the word heavy with meaning. "The rebirth of a planet, of a species, of everything they've lost touch with."

"Yes. But you'll forget, too," her Self reminded her. "When you arrive, you'll be as human as the rest. You'll have to rediscover the truths you already know."

Aria's gaze shifted to the empty space around them, filled with endless potential. "I've forgotten before," she said, her voice soft. "But I always find my way back. That's the beauty of it, isn't it? We forget, and then we remember. Over and over again."

Her Self leaned back, arms crossed behind its head, looking far too relaxed for someone discussing the fate of an entire planet. "And then we get to play more tic-tac-toe."

Aria snorted. "Maybe next time, we'll try chess again."

The being's eyes twinkled with amusement. "Ah, yes. A game of strategy and surrender. Very fitting for the journey ahead."

For a moment, they sat in comfortable silence, the vastness of eternity stretching out before them, filled with endless possibilities. The tic-tac-toe board vanished, replaced by the quiet hum of the universe itself.

"You're ready," her Self said, the playfulness gone, replaced with a deep, unwavering certainty. "It's time."

Aria nodded, feeling the pull of Earth, the pull of life, calling her back. "I'm ready."

As she stood, preparing to leave the timeless space and descend once more into the world of form, her Self reached out and touched her hand. "Remember, Aria. The game isn't about winning. It's about love. Always love."

Aria smiled, her heart full. "I won't forget. Not this time."

Her Self winked, the grin back in full force. "You always say that."

With one last glance at the infinite space around her, Aria stepped forward, into the light, into the unknown, into the Re-Genesis.

The game would begin again.

But this time, Aria knew the rules.

Part One

THE WINDOW OF EXISTENCE

1

The Dance of Infinity

Aria stood at the threshold of existence, suspended between the vastness of eternity and the quiet pull of her next life. Around her, time didn't flow the way it did on Earth. There were no seconds, no minutes, no hours—only the endless hum of infinity, stretching out in every direction.

Infinity felt different here, like a living force, pulsating and weaving through the fabric of everything. Aria wasn't just observing it—she was *in* it, part of it. The concept of "before" and "after" didn't make sense here. There was no beginning, no end, just the eternal dance of creation, destruction, and rebirth.

As she hovered in this timeless space, her mind drifted through the cycles of existence she had experienced. Lives lived in every form imaginable—human, animal, even the elements. She had been a drop of rain, a flame flickering in the darkness, a gust of wind sweeping through the trees. She had been the stars themselves, and yet each time, she returned to this place.

"This is what infinity feels like," she whispered, watching as the shimmering strands of existence wove themselves around her. "Endless. Unfolding. And always in motion."

The voice of her Self, ever-present, echoed softly through the ether. "Infinity is a paradox, isn't it? It's everything, and yet, nothing at all. No beginning, no end. Just... *being*."

Aria nodded. She could feel the truth of those words deep in her bones. Infinity wasn't something to be understood by the mind. It could only be felt. Experienced. Like a river that flows forever, without ever reaching a destination.

"Why do we keep coming back to this place?" Aria asked, her voice soft, as if she didn't want to disturb the peace of the moment.

Her Self appeared beside her, this time in the form of a swirling, golden mist. It shimmered and danced, just like the infinite space around them.

"Because it's where we're from," the mist answered, its voice light and teasing, as though it was answering a riddle she already knew. "This is where we start, and this is where we return. It's home."

Aria floated through the mist, her mind spinning with thoughts of infinity. She had been here before, countless times, but it always felt new. Each return was different, each cycle a little more nuanced than the last. Infinity wasn't stagnant. It was constantly shifting, evolving, becoming.

"I can feel it," she said, watching as the strands of time and space twisted and braided themselves together in front of her. "Everything is connected. Every moment, every thought, every action… it's all part of the same dance."

Her Self laughed softly, the sound like a breeze rustling through the cosmos. "That's the beauty of it, Aria. There's no separation. Every life you've lived, every choice you've made, every person you've been—it's all woven into the same tapestry."

Aria closed her eyes, allowing herself to drift deeper into the flow of infinity. She could feel the pulse of creation, the constant rhythm of birth and rebirth. She had lived so many lives, each one a new chapter in the endless book of existence. And yet, no matter how many times she returned, the dance of infinity remained a mystery.

"What's the point of it all?" she asked, her voice barely above a whisper. "Why do we keep coming back? Why do we keep forgetting?"

Her Self materialized beside her again, this time in the form of her reflection—a mirror image of Aria, but with a mischievous glint in her eyes. "Ah, that's the eternal question, isn't it? The truth is, you come back to remember. To learn. To grow. And each time you forget, it's because the forgetting is part of the learning."

Aria's brow furrowed, trying to wrap her mind around the paradox. "So... we forget so we can remember?"

Her Self grinned, as if Aria had just stumbled upon a great cosmic joke. "Exactly. Without the forgetting, there's no journey. And without the journey, there's no growth."

Aria sighed, but there was a smile tugging at her lips. "I suppose that makes sense, in an infinite sort of way."

The strands of time and space danced around her, weaving themselves into patterns too intricate for the human mind to comprehend. Aria watched them with a sense of wonder. The cycles of existence, the birth and death of stars, the rise and fall of civilizations—it was all part of the same cosmic dance. Each moment connected to the next, each life a thread in the tapestry of the universe.

"Infinity is never still," her Self said, swirling around her like the breeze. "It's always in motion, always becoming something new. And so are you."

Aria floated through the vastness, her mind still lingering on the idea of infinity. She had spent so much of her previous lives trying to understand it—trying to grasp the meaning behind it all. But here, in this place beyond time, she realized that there was no single meaning. Infinity wasn't something that could be understood. It was something to be *lived*.

The mist swirled around her, and her Self's voice softened, as if sharing a secret. "You're part of the dance, Aria. Just like every star, every galaxy, every life. And just like them, you're always becoming something more."

Aria smiled, feeling the weight of those words settle in her heart. She had always been searching for meaning, always trying to find her place in the universe. But now, she saw that her place wasn't something to find—it was something she was creating with every step, every choice, every life.

"I'm not looking for answers anymore," she said quietly. "I'm just... part of the dance."

Her Self beamed, the mist swirling with approval. "Now you're getting it. You don't have to figure everything out. Just keep moving, keep becoming. Infinity will take care of the rest."

Aria laughed softly, the sound mingling with the hum of the cosmos. The dance of infinity was all around her, and she was finally ready to let herself be part of it.

As she floated through the endless space, she felt a gentle pull—an invitation to return to the world of form. It was time to begin again, to step into a new life, a new journey.

But this time, she wasn't afraid. This time, she wasn't searching for meaning or answers. She was ready to embrace the cycles, the forgetting, the remembering. She was ready to dance.

Her Self drifted beside her, its voice a whisper in the wind. "Are you ready, Aria?"

She nodded, her heart full of peace. "I'm ready."

With one last glance at the infinite space around her, Aria took a deep breath and stepped forward, into the flow of existence, into the Dance of Infinity.

2

Beyond the Game

Aria hovered in the space between thoughts, between lives, wrapped in the infinite stillness that surrounded her. Yet even here, in this boundless expanse, there was a subtle tension—something pulling at her from the depths of creation. A reminder that her journey wasn't done.

And then, just as suddenly, her Self appeared again. This time it took the shape of a casual, laid-back version of Aria herself, sitting on a floating couch in the middle of the void, feet propped up on an invisible table. A deck of cards shuffled themselves in the air in front of it, flipping lazily as her Self eyed her with a knowing smile.

"You've thought about infinity," her Self began, "but there's more to the story. Games, rules, paradoxes—you're still caught up in them."

Aria raised an eyebrow, amused. "Games? We just finished playing tic-tac-toe, remember? I think I've had enough."

Her Self smirked. "Oh, that little thing? Tic-tac-toe is just a warm-up, darling. The real game is much bigger. You've been playing it for lifetimes, and guess what? The rules don't work the way you think they do."

The cards in the air flipped, rearranged, and snapped into a perfect stack, hovering just beyond her Self's hand. Aria tilted her head, intrigued but cautious. "You're saying I've been playing a game without knowing the rules?"

"Exactly." Her Self winked, drawing a card from the deck and holding it up. "The paradox of existence. You spend your whole life trying to figure it out—trying to make sense of what's real and what's not. But guess what? The rules aren't fixed. They bend."

Aria studied the card. It was blank. No markings, no numbers. Just an empty space where meaning should be. "A game with no rules. How do you play?"

Her Self leaned back, shrugging. "That's the fun of it. You don't. Not in the way you're used to. The trick is, the more you try to control the game, the more it slips through your fingers. But when you stop trying to win? That's when you really start playing."

Aria frowned, the idea teasing the edges of her understanding. She had spent lifetimes striving—chasing success, control, love. Always moving forward, always thinking she could *figure it out*. But now, sitting in this timeless space, she began to wonder if she had been going about it all wrong.

"Let me guess," she said, her voice softening, "I've been trying to control the game, when I should've been letting it unfold."

Her Self gave her a slow, approving nod, as if Aria had just solved an ancient riddle. "Bingo. You've been caught up in the idea that life is something to be mastered. That there's a strategy. That if you just play your cards right, you'll finally win. But that's the paradox. The moment you stop playing to win, you realize there's no need to win at all. It's not about the destination, Aria. It's about the experience."

The deck of cards shuffled again, each one flipping and twisting in midair before returning to the stack. Aria watched them, her mind churning with the implications. She had spent so much time in her past lives trying to make sense of things. Trying to master herself, to master her environment, to achieve some final goal—whether it was enlightenment, love, or control. But now, sitting here with her Self, it seemed so obvious.

"The game isn't about winning," Aria said softly, more to herself than to her Self. "It's about playing."

Her Self clapped its hands together, beaming with delight. "Yes! Exactly. You've been thinking of life like chess—strategy, rules, winners, and losers. But it's not like that. Life is more like…" Her Self paused, flipping a card into the air where it spun lazily before disappearing. "More like a dance. No winners. No losers. Just movement."

Aria leaned back, exhaling as the weight of that realization settled over her. "So, all this time I've spent trying to control things… it's been useless?"

Her Self laughed, a sound that sparkled through the air like the chiming of bells. "Not useless. Just unnecessary. You see, Aria, control is a nice illusion. It keeps you feeling safe. It makes you think you're steering the ship. But the truth is, the game doesn't need you to steer it. Life flows whether you're controlling it or not. In fact, it flows *better* when you're not trying to control it."

Aria felt her thoughts unraveling, the tightly wound threads of her desire for control loosening, slipping through her fingers. She had spent lifetimes trying to understand the paradoxes of existence. Trying to figure out how to live in a world that seemed full of chaos, uncertainty, and confusion. But maybe… maybe the answer wasn't in figuring it out at all. Maybe the answer was in letting it be.

"So, I just… let go?" Aria asked, a bit of doubt creeping into her voice. "That's it? No plan, no strategy?"

Her Self nodded, grinning. "Exactly. You let go. You trust the flow of the game. You allow yourself to move with it, rather than against it."

Aria sat quietly, absorbing this. Letting go was easier said than done. She had spent so long believing she had to *do* something, that she had to play by certain rules in order to achieve her goals. But now, here, in this space beyond time and existence, she could see how futile that effort had been.

"And what about purpose?" Aria asked, her mind still clinging to the one thing that had always driven her forward. "If we're just playing, what about purpose? Don't we need a reason?"

Her Self's eyes twinkled with mischief. "Purpose? Of course, you have a purpose. Everyone does. But here's the twist: purpose isn't a goal to be achieved. It's a way of being. It's not something you reach at the end of the game. It's something you live *through* the game."

Aria tilted her head, trying to wrap her mind around this new concept. Purpose wasn't an endpoint—it was woven into the fabric of every moment. Every choice, every action, every breath. "So, purpose is how we *play*?"

Her Self smiled softly, watching her with a kind of cosmic affection. "Yes, Aria. Purpose is the way you engage with life, not something you chase after. When you live with purpose, it's not because you're trying to win. It's because you're fully present in the game. Every move you make, every step you take—it's filled with intention. Not to reach some end, but because that's how the game is meant to be played."

Aria's heart fluttered with the simplicity of the truth. Life wasn't a race, or a strategy game, or a puzzle to solve. It was an endless, flowing dance, and the only way to truly experience it was to let go of the need to control it.

She exhaled, feeling the tension she'd carried for lifetimes slowly melt away. "Let go," she whispered, her words like a promise to herself. "Live through the game. Play, not to win, but to experience."

Her Self nodded, the golden mist around it shimmering as it began to dissolve back into the infinite space. "You're getting closer, Aria. You're beginning to understand."

Aria smiled, her heart light. "Thank you."

Her Self grinned one last time, then winked. "Anytime. Now go on, enjoy the game. And remember—you're always free to bend the rules."

With that, her Self disappeared, leaving Aria alone in the vastness of existence. But she didn't feel alone. She felt… connected. To the game, to the flow of life, to everything.

She looked around at the infinite space surrounding her, but instead of feeling lost, she felt free. Free to play, free to live, free to move through life without the need for answers or control.

The game was still unfolding, and Aria was ready.

This time, she wasn't playing to win.

She was playing to live.

3

Re-Genesis Revealed

Aria drifted through the infinite space, feeling lighter than she had in lifetimes. The need to control, the constant push for answers—gone. All that remained was the quiet pulse of existence and the sense that something new was on the horizon.

A soft pull began to tug at her, as if the universe itself was guiding her to a new truth. She let herself follow, allowing the current to carry her. The space around her shifted, the shimmering vastness morphing into something more tangible. Ahead, she saw a vision taking shape—an ancient tree with roots that stretched deep into the earth and branches that reached into the cosmos.

This was no ordinary tree. Its bark shimmered with a silver hue, glowing with the light of a thousand stars. Leaves sparkled like galaxies, shifting in patterns that defied logic. At the center of the tree, a soft glow pulsed, calling to her.

Her Self reappeared beside her, leaning casually against the tree, the playful grin back in place. "You've reached the Re-Genesis tree," it said, voice light but filled with significance.

"Re-Genesis," Aria repeated, her gaze locked on the glowing core of the tree. "What is it?"

Her Self crossed its arms, leaning in with a conspiratorial air. "Re-Genesis is the moment when everything starts again. But this time, it's not just about *you*. It's about the world, humanity, the universe itself. It's the restart of the cosmic game, but on a much bigger scale."

Aria blinked, stepping closer to the tree. The air around it seemed to hum with energy, vibrating with potential. "A restart? Like a reset button for existence?"

Her Self laughed softly. "Not exactly. It's more like a rebirth, a renewal of all that is. Humanity is standing on the edge of something new. They're lost in conflict, war, division, and they've forgotten the essence of who they are. But Re-Genesis will bring a new beginning—a chance for them to wake up, to remember."

Aria touched the bark of the tree, feeling the energy pulse beneath her fingers. It was alive, brimming with power. The possibilities swirled around her, infinite and yet all tied to this single point in time.

"Why now?" Aria asked. "Why is the Re-Genesis happening now?"

Her Self leaned forward, eyes sparkling with wisdom. "Because humanity is at a tipping point. The love of power has clouded the power of love. They've lost sight of the truth—of who they are. But every ending gives way to a new beginning. This is that beginning."

Aria's mind flickered back to Earth, to the chaos and division she had seen in her many lives. The wars, the hatred, the fear. Humanity had been trapped in cycles of conflict for so long, unable to see that they were fighting themselves. She had seen the same story play out across generations, across different lives. Always the same, always repeating.

But now... now there was a chance to break the cycle.

"Re-Genesis," she said softly, her fingers still resting on the glowing tree. "A chance to start over. To create something new."

Her Self nodded, stepping beside her to gaze at the tree. "Exactly. But here's the thing—this time, the change won't come from outside. It has to come from within. Humanity isn't just going to wake up one day and realize everything's different. They have to be reminded. They have to remember who they are."

Aria felt a surge of energy pass through her as she understood what her Self was saying. This wasn't just a reset for the world. It was a re-awakening of consciousness, a shift in the way people saw themselves and each other. They needed to remember the connection between all things—the oneness that existed beneath the surface of separation.

"And that's where I come in," Aria realized, her voice steady with new understanding.

Her Self smiled, a soft warmth radiating from it. "You always were quick on the uptake."

Aria laughed, the sound blending with the hum of the tree. "So, my purpose is to help them remember. To guide them through the Re-Genesis."

"Not just your purpose," her Self corrected gently, "but your *gift*. You've been through lifetimes of learning, of experiencing both the light and the shadow, and now it's time to bring that knowledge to others. The Re-Genesis isn't just a new start—it's a chance for everyone to evolve. But they can't do it without remembering their true essence."

Aria felt a deep sense of responsibility settle over her, but it wasn't heavy or burdensome. It felt right. It felt like the culmination of everything she had experienced in her countless lives. She had been learning, growing, evolving—and now it was time to share that with the world.

Her gaze shifted back to the glowing center of the tree. "How do I do it? How do I help them remember?"

Her Self stepped closer, resting a hand on her shoulder. "By embodying the truth yourself. By living with love, with purpose, with awareness of the oneness that connects everything. When you live that truth, others will begin to see it in themselves. It's not about forcing change—it's about being the change. When you shine your light, you make it easier for others to find their own."

Aria closed her eyes, feeling the weight of her Self's words. She had always known, on some level, that her purpose was to help others, but now it felt clearer than ever. The world was on the edge of something monumental, and she was part of that shift. The Re-Genesis was coming, and it wasn't just about saving the world—it was about waking it up.

"So, I just... live with love? That's it?" she asked, her voice full of quiet wonder.

Her Self laughed softly. "It sounds simple, doesn't it? But that's the beauty of it. Love *is* simple. It's the most powerful force in the universe, and yet it's the one thing humanity has forgotten. When they remember love—true, unconditional love—the Re-Genesis will unfold naturally."

Aria stood still, absorbing the magnitude of what lay ahead. The weight of her purpose felt different now, not as a burden, but as a gift. She had the power to help the world remember. Not through force, but through love. Through her own light.

"You're ready," her Self said softly, stepping back from the tree. "You've been ready for lifetimes. This is just the next step."

Aria nodded, her heart steady, her mind clear. She was ready. She had been preparing for this moment, for this new beginning, through every life she had lived. And now, it was time to step into her purpose fully.

The tree pulsed with light, glowing brighter as if it, too, was ready for the Re-Genesis to begin.

"Remember, Aria," her Self said, its voice a soft echo in the vastness of existence, "it's not about changing the world. It's about helping them remember they're already part of the light."

Aria smiled, her heart swelling with love, with purpose, with the quiet certainty that she was exactly where she needed to be.

The Re-Genesis was coming. And Aria was ready to help the world wake up.

Part Two

THE OTHER LIFE

4

Witnessing the Other

The stillness of infinity gave way, and Aria found herself floating in a new space—no longer in the timeless realm of existence, but somewhere softer, warmer. She could feel the pulse of life around her, the rhythms of time and motion returning as she drifted closer to the world of form.

A soft golden light enveloped her, and slowly, a vision began to take shape. It was familiar and unfamiliar all at once, a place rooted in the human world but tinged with the ethereal. She was witnessing another life, but it wasn't hers. Not exactly. It belonged to someone else—someone deeply connected to her, yet separate.

As the vision became clearer, Aria saw a person sitting alone at a small table, hunched over a cup of tea that had long since gone cold. The room around them was dimly lit, cluttered with books, half-written notes, and objects that hinted at a life searching for meaning. A flickering candle cast long shadows on the walls, dancing as if they had stories to tell.

The person—whom Aria could only think of as *the Other*—sighed deeply, running a hand through their hair, lost in thought. Their face, though not yet fully visible to Aria, carried the weight of someone who had been searching for a long time. There was a quiet sadness there, a longing for something more, something just out of reach.

Aria drifted closer, observing the scene with a mixture of curiosity and empathy. Who was this person? Why was she being shown this life?

Her Self appeared beside her, this time as a glowing orb of light, gently pulsing in rhythm with the scene before them.

"Who is this?" Aria asked, her voice soft, not wanting to disturb the quiet moment.

Her Self hovered beside her, its light warm and calming. "This is the Other. They are you, in a way—but also not you."

Aria frowned, watching as the Other stared blankly into the flickering candle, their eyes distant, as though lost in a world of unanswered questions. "What do you mean, 'they are me'? I don't recognize them."

"You will," her Self replied, its voice filled with quiet certainty. "This life is deeply connected to yours. They are on their own journey, much like you've been on yours. But they are searching for something—something they can't quite grasp. They feel disconnected, from themselves and from the world."

Aria continued to watch, her heart aching as she felt the Other's quiet frustration. The room around them seemed to reflect their inner state—cluttered, disorganized, full of unfinished thoughts and projects. Books were piled high on the table, each one marked with half-read pages. Notes were scrawled on bits of paper, but none seemed complete. There was an air of restlessness, of longing.

"They're searching for meaning," Aria whispered, almost to herself. "They want something more."

Her Self's light pulsed softly. "Yes. They feel lost, as many do. But their search is sincere. They want to make a difference in the world, to help others, but they don't know how. They're overwhelmed by their own uncertainty."

Aria's chest tightened with empathy. She could feel the weight of the Other's emotions—the longing, the frustration, the desire to do something meaningful, but not knowing where to start. It was a familiar feeling, one she had encountered in her own journey through life.

"What are they looking for?" Aria asked, her voice filled with compassion.

"They're looking for purpose," her Self replied. "But they think of purpose as something external, something they need to find outside of themselves. They're searching for validation, for proof that they matter."

Aria watched as the Other picked up one of the books from the table, flipping through the pages absentmindedly. Their brow furrowed, and they set it down again with a frustrated sigh. It was clear they were seeking answers, but the answers weren't coming from the books or the notes or the candlelight flickering before them.

Aria felt a deep connection to this person, even though they remained a stranger. She could see parts of herself reflected in their struggle—in the way they reached for meaning but felt like it slipped through their fingers.

"They're so close," Aria murmured, watching as the Other stared into the flame, as though hoping it would reveal some hidden truth. "They're right on the edge of understanding."

Her Self hummed softly in agreement. "Yes, they are. But they haven't yet realized that the answers they seek are already within them. They're too busy looking outward, trying to find purpose in things, in achievements, in recognition from others."

The Other shifted in their seat, rubbing their temples as though trying to force clarity. Aria could feel their exhaustion—the tiredness that came from searching for meaning in places where it couldn't be found. The clutter around them was symbolic of the clutter in their mind, filled with distractions and half-formed ideas.

"What can I do?" Aria asked, her voice filled with quiet urgency. "How can I help them?"

Her Self's light brightened for a moment, casting a warm glow over the scene. "For now, you are simply here to witness. You cannot force their awakening, Aria. You can only be a guide when they are ready to see."

Aria nodded slowly, her heart heavy with the realization that she couldn't save the Other from their struggle. She couldn't give them the answers they were so desperately seeking. That wasn't how it worked.

She watched as the Other leaned back in their chair, closing their eyes for a moment, the weight of their own search pressing down on them. There was so much beauty in their soul, so much light waiting to be uncovered, but it was hidden beneath layers of doubt, fear, and uncertainty.

"They have so much to give," Aria whispered, feeling the stirrings of hope for the Other. "They just don't see it yet."

Her Self drifted closer, the light warm and comforting. "Yes. They will see it in time. But first, they must let go of the idea that their worth is tied to their achievements. They must realize that their purpose isn't something they have to *find*—it's something they already *are*."

Aria watched the Other, feeling the depth of their internal struggle. She understood now why she was being shown this life. It wasn't about witnessing someone else's journey—it was about seeing a reflection of the human condition. The Other represented more than just one life—they represented the collective search for meaning that so many people experienced.

"They're not alone," Aria said softly, more to herself than to her Self. "So many people feel this way. So many people are searching, just like them."

Her Self pulsed with quiet agreement. "Yes. And that's why the Re-Genesis is so important. It's time for humanity to remember that they don't need to search for meaning outside themselves. The answers are already within."

Aria nodded, her heart swelling with compassion for the Other and for all those who felt the same way. The Re-Genesis wasn't just about a cosmic restart—it was about helping people wake up to the truth of who they were, to the light that was already inside them.

The Other opened their eyes, staring into the flickering candle once again. For a moment, a glimmer of something crossed their face—perhaps the beginnings of realization, or maybe just a moment of peace in the midst of their search.

Aria watched, hopeful, as the vision began to fade, the scene dissolving into the golden light that surrounded her.

"They're close," her Self whispered, its voice filled with quiet certainty. "And when they're ready, you will be there to guide them."

Aria nodded, feeling the weight of that responsibility settle over her, but it wasn't a burden. It was a gift—a chance to help others remember the truth of their own existence.

As the vision faded completely, Aria was left with a deep sense of connection to the Other and to humanity as a whole. She had witnessed their journey, and now, she was ready to play her part in helping them find their way back to the light.

The Re-Genesis was beginning.

And Aria would be there, every step of the way.

5

The Beauty of Flaws

The vision of the Other lingered in Aria's mind like a half-forgotten dream, their struggles and quiet yearning for meaning woven into the fabric of her thoughts. As she drifted through the space of infinite possibilities, the golden light that surrounded her pulsed gently, like a heartbeat guiding her forward. She had witnessed their restlessness, their search for purpose. But now, it was time to look deeper—to see beyond the surface and understand the beauty that lay hidden beneath their flaws.

The world around her shifted again, and soon, Aria found herself back in the presence of the Other. The scene was different this time—more intimate, more alive. The room was the same, cluttered with books and papers, but there was a new energy in the air. The Other sat at the same table, but now their hands were moving—busy, focused, creating.

Aria hovered near the edge of the scene, watching as the Other worked on a project, piecing together fragments of wood and metal into something vaguely recognizable. Their brow was furrowed in concentration, their lips slightly pursed as they studied the pieces before them. There was an intensity in their movements, a drive to create something meaningful, even if they weren't entirely sure what that something was.

"They're trying so hard," Aria murmured, a soft smile touching her lips. "They think they need to get everything right."

Her Self appeared beside her, this time in the form of a glowing figure that shimmered like the stars. It radiated warmth and light, a calming presence that made the chaotic scene before them seem less daunting.

"Of course they do," her Self replied, voice laced with affection. "They've been conditioned to believe that perfection is the goal. That flaws are something to fix."

Aria watched as the Other paused in their work, their hands hovering over the scattered materials on the table. A quiet sigh escaped their lips, and for a moment, their shoulders slumped, as if the weight of their own expectations had become too much to carry.

"They see their flaws as failures," Aria whispered, her heart aching for them. "They think they're not good enough."

Her Self nodded gently. "It's the way of most humans, isn't it? They measure themselves by their mistakes, by what they think they lack. But they forget that their flaws are what make them beautiful."

Aria tilted her head, her eyes fixed on the Other's face. There was so much vulnerability there, so much desire to be better, to be *enough*. And yet, in their quiet frustration, Aria could see something else—something that the Other couldn't see in themselves.

"They're... so human," Aria said softly, her voice filled with wonder. "So imperfect, but in a way that's so... real. So genuine."

Her Self's light shimmered brighter for a moment, as if reflecting the truth in Aria's words. "Yes. And that's the beauty of it. Their flaws aren't something to be fixed—they're part of who they are. They give them depth, character. They make them unique."

Aria continued to watch as the Other resumed their work, this time with a little more determination. The project wasn't going smoothly. Pieces didn't fit together perfectly, and there were moments of hesitation, where the Other clearly doubted their abilities. But they kept going, despite the frustration, despite the doubt.

"There's a kind of beauty in that," Aria mused. "In the way they keep trying, even when they think they're failing."

Her Self drifted closer, its presence a comforting glow beside her. "That's what makes them strong, even though they don't see it. Their flaws, their mistakes—those are the things that push them to grow. Without them, there would be no reason to evolve, no reason to seek something more."

Aria smiled, a deep sense of understanding settling over her. She had spent so many lifetimes in search of perfection herself—trying to master life, trying to get everything right. But now, as she watched the Other, she realized that the journey wasn't about being perfect. It was about embracing the imperfections, the flaws, the moments of doubt. Because in those moments, that was where the real growth happened.

"They don't need to be perfect," Aria said, her voice filled with quiet certainty. "They just need to keep going."

Her Self's light pulsed in agreement. "Exactly. It's the journey, not the destination. Their flaws are what make the journey interesting. What would life be if everything were perfect, if there were no mistakes to learn from?"

Aria thought about that for a moment, the weight of the question sinking in. A life without mistakes, without flaws—what would that even look like? The idea felt hollow, empty. Without challenges, without moments of failure, there would be no growth, no discovery, no reason to strive for anything.

As if sensing her thoughts, the Other paused again, this time looking down at their hands. A piece of wood they had been working with had splintered, the edges jagged and uneven. For a moment, the Other stared at it in frustration, their face creasing with disappointment. But then, something shifted. Their expression softened, and instead of discarding the piece, they picked it up and began to work with it—gently, carefully, shaping it into something new.

Aria's heart swelled with quiet pride as she watched the transformation unfold. The Other wasn't giving up. They weren't throwing away their flawed creation. They were finding a way to make it part of the whole, to use the imperfection to create something more meaningful.

"They're learning," Aria said softly, a smile tugging at her lips. "They're starting to see that their flaws don't define them."

Her Self's light shimmered with approval. "Yes. And that's the lesson they need to learn—not just them, but all of humanity. The Re-Genesis is about more than just starting over. It's about embracing the flaws, the imperfections, and realizing that those are the very things that make life beautiful."

Aria nodded, her heart full of understanding. The Other, like so many others, had been conditioned to believe that their worth was tied to their perfection. That their value depended on how well they could avoid mistakes, how flawlessly they could perform. But that wasn't the truth. The truth was that their flaws were part of what made them who they were—part of what made them human.

"They're so much more than their flaws," Aria whispered, her eyes softening as she watched the Other work. "They just need to see it."

Her Self's voice was gentle, filled with warmth. "And they will. In time, they will."

As the scene before her began to fade, Aria felt a deep sense of connection to the Other and to the journey they were on. She understood now that their flaws weren't something to be ashamed of—they were part of the process, part of the evolution of the soul. And in that understanding, she felt a quiet sense of peace.

"They don't need to be perfect," she said, her voice filled with love. "They just need to keep going."

And as the vision dissolved into golden light, Aria knew that the Other—and all those like them—would find their way. Not by chasing perfection, but by embracing the beauty of their flaws.

Because in the end, it was their imperfections that made them whole.

6

The Search for Sacred Purpose

Aria lingered in the golden light, the image of the Other still fresh in her mind. Their struggle had touched her deeply—the way they had searched, reached, and grasped for something just beyond their understanding. She could feel their longing for purpose, that deep yearning to belong, to make a difference, to find meaning in the chaos. It was a familiar ache, one she had known in her own journey through lifetimes.

As the scene around her shifted once more, Aria found herself drawn back to the Other's life. This time, she was not in their cluttered, cozy room but in a larger world—a world bustling with activity and sound, a world of distractions and desires. The Other stood in the middle of it all, surrounded by people, but somehow entirely alone.

Aria hovered nearby, watching the scene unfold with quiet empathy. The Other walked through the streets of a busy city, their steps hurried but directionless. People brushed past them, each one absorbed in their own lives, their own goals, their own needs. The world around them felt fast-paced, chaotic, like everyone was rushing toward something—but what, exactly, no one seemed to know.

The Other, too, was rushing. Their eyes darted from one thing to the next—billboards advertising success, people laughing in cafes, newsstands filled with stories of triumph and failure. Everywhere they looked, there were signs pointing to what they *should* be, what they *should* do, who they *should* become. But none of it felt real. None of it felt like the truth they were searching for.

"They're lost," Aria whispered, her heart aching as she watched the Other push through the crowds. "They want something real, something meaningful."

Her Self appeared beside her, this time as a figure of shimmering light, its features soft and gentle. "They're searching for sacred purpose," her Self replied, its voice calm and full of understanding. "But they're looking for it in the wrong places."

Aria nodded, watching as the Other paused in front of a grand building, its windows gleaming with promise. The sign above the door read *Success Starts Here*, and for a moment, the Other hesitated, as though considering stepping inside. But they didn't. Instead, they turned away, their shoulders slumping in quiet defeat.

"They think purpose is something they have to achieve," Aria said, her voice filled with quiet sadness. "Something they have to *earn*."

Her Self hummed softly, a sound like the rustling of leaves in a gentle breeze. "That's what most people believe, isn't it? That purpose is something they have to chase. That it's something external, something they can only find once they've reached a certain level of success, or wealth, or recognition."

The Other continued walking, their steps slower now, more uncertain. They passed by people who seemed confident, self-assured, as though they knew exactly where they were going, exactly what they were doing with their lives. And each time the Other saw someone like that, their sense of inadequacy deepened, their longing for purpose growing more desperate.

"They don't see it," Aria murmured, her eyes fixed on the Other. "They don't see that purpose isn't something out there."

Her Self's light pulsed gently. "No, they don't. Not yet. They're too caught up in the idea that their purpose is something they have to discover, something they have to *become*. But the truth is, purpose is already within them."

Aria could feel the weight of that truth settle over her. She had seen it in the Other—the way they had searched so earnestly, the way they had tried to mold themselves into something that fit the world's expectations. They had believed that if they could just *find* their purpose, everything would fall into place. But they had been looking in the wrong direction, searching outward when the answers were already within.

"They're trying so hard," Aria whispered, her heart aching for the Other. "But they don't realize that their purpose is already part of who they are."

Her Self drifted closer, its presence warm and reassuring. "It's a common mistake. Humans often believe that purpose is something grand, something world-changing. They think it's tied to their achievements, their status, their impact on the world. But real purpose—sacred purpose—isn't about what you do. It's about who you *are*."

Aria's gaze softened as she watched the Other. They had stopped walking now, standing at the edge of a small park, watching children play and people chat on benches. There was a quiet sadness in their posture, a sense of being disconnected from the joy around them. They wanted so desperately to belong, to contribute, to find their place in the world—but they didn't know how.

"They're looking for something big," Aria said softly. "Something that will give their life meaning."

Her Self nodded, its light flickering like a candle in the dark. "But sacred purpose isn't always big, Aria. It's not about changing the world in some grand way. It's about living with intention, with love, with authenticity. It's about being true to yourself, and in doing so, inspiring others to do the same."

Aria watched as the Other sat down on a bench, their head in their hands, lost in their own thoughts. She could feel their frustration, their sense of failure, as though they believed they were missing something essential, something that everyone else seemed to have. But what they didn't see—what Aria could see so clearly—was that their purpose was already within them. It had been all along.

"They don't need to become anything," Aria said, her voice filled with quiet certainty. "They just need to *be*."

Her Self's light brightened, a soft glow of approval. "Exactly. But that's the hardest lesson of all, isn't it? To accept that you are already enough. That your purpose isn't tied to what you achieve, but to how you live, how you love, how you connect with others."

Aria nodded, feeling the truth of those words resonate deep within her. She had seen it in the Other—the way they had searched for meaning in all the wrong places, the way they had compared themselves to others, believing that their worth was tied to their accomplishments. But purpose wasn't something that could be measured by external success. It was something far more personal, far more sacred.

"They'll figure it out," Aria said softly, her heart full of compassion. "They'll find their way."

Her Self's voice was warm, filled with quiet assurance. "Yes, they will. But it won't come from chasing after purpose. It will come from within. It will come when they stop trying to *become* something, and start embracing who they already are."

Aria watched as the Other lifted their head, their eyes scanning the park with a quiet sense of wonder. The children playing, the couples walking hand in hand, the people laughing together—it wasn't grand or world-changing, but it was full of meaning. Full of connection.

The Other stood up, their steps slower now, more deliberate. There was a shift in their energy, a subtle realization that perhaps, just perhaps, the answers they were seeking weren't as far away as they thought.

"They're starting to see it," Aria whispered, a smile tugging at her lips. "They're starting to understand."

Her Self's light shimmered beside her, a soft glow of approval. "Yes. And when they finally let go of the need to find purpose, that's when they'll discover it. Purpose isn't about doing something extraordinary, Aria. It's about living with love, with kindness, with the awareness that every moment, every interaction, is sacred."

Aria's heart swelled with understanding. The Other's journey was a reflection of so many people's journeys—the search for meaning, the desire to contribute, the longing for purpose. But in that search, they often missed the most important truth: that purpose wasn't something to be found. It was something to be *lived*.

As the scene before her began to fade, Aria felt a deep sense of peace settle over her. The Other was on their path, just as she had been on hers. They would find their way, not by chasing after some distant goal, but by embracing the beauty of who they already were.

"The Re-Genesis is about remembering," Aria said softly, her voice filled with quiet conviction. "Remembering that we are enough, just as we are."

Her Self's light pulsed gently, a final affirmation before the vision dissolved into golden light.

"Yes," her Self whispered, its voice full of love. "That's the truth they're searching for. And one day, they will remember."

And as the golden light enveloped her, Aria knew that when the Other found their sacred purpose, it wouldn't be in some grand achievement or world-changing act. It would be in the quiet moments of love, of connection, of simply being.

Because in the end, purpose wasn't something to be found.

It was something to be *lived*.

Part Three

THE REFLECTION

7

The Cosmic Mirror

The golden light faded around Aria, leaving her in a space that felt both familiar and new. She stood in a vast, shimmering void, not quite like the infinite expanse she had traversed before. This place was different. It was alive with potential, filled with reflections that rippled like the surface of water, shimmering with unseen truths just below the surface.

Aria had seen these reflections before—glimpses of lives, choices, and paths she had walked in her many lifetimes. But this time, as she gazed into the endless reflections around her, she sensed something deeper. These weren't just echoes of her past. There was something more—something she had missed.

Her Self appeared beside her, still glowing with a soft light, but its form now more abstract, less human than before. It hovered beside her, a presence of warmth and guidance.

"You're starting to see it," her Self said, voice calm and steady. "This isn't just about the Other. It's about all of us. It's about you."

Aria furrowed her brow, turning to the nearest reflection. The surface rippled, and in its depths, she saw the Other again—walking through the city, sitting at the bench, staring into the candlelight. They looked just as lost, just as searching as before, but there was something different about the way Aria saw them now.

"They're me," Aria whispered, the realization dawning on her. "Aren't they? They're... a reflection of me."

Her Self shimmered, its light pulsing softly. "Yes. You and the Other, you are not so separate. Their journey mirrors your own. Just as their search for purpose is a reflection of the human experience, it's also a reflection of your own."

Aria stared into the reflection, her heart racing as the truth settled over her like a blanket. She had felt so connected to the Other's struggle, their search for meaning, their longing to find their place in the world—and now she understood why. They were not just another life, another individual on their own path. They were an aspect of herself.

"Everything is connected," Aria said softly, her voice filled with wonder. "Every life, every journey... it's all part of the same whole."

Her Self drifted closer, its light merging with the reflections around them. "That's the truth you've been seeking. The lives you've lived, the people you've been, the paths you've walked—they're all part of a greater tapestry. The Other is just one thread in that tapestry. You've been witnessing yourself, through them."

Aria's mind spun with the implications. She had always known, on some level, that there was a connection between all beings, a shared oneness that ran beneath the surface of life. But now, standing before this cosmic mirror, she could see it with perfect clarity. The Other's search for purpose was her own search. Their doubts, their fears, their longing for meaning—these were the same struggles she had faced in every lifetime.

She reached out, her hand brushing against the surface of the reflection. It rippled beneath her fingers, and as it did, she saw the image change. It was no longer the Other sitting on the bench, but *her*. Aria herself, from another lifetime—sitting in a different place, in a different body, but with the same expression of quiet longing on her face. The same search for purpose, the same desire to know who she truly was.

"I've been searching for myself," Aria whispered, the weight of the realization settling in her chest. "All this time, through every life, every experience... I've been trying to find myself."

Her Self nodded, its light reflecting the quiet understanding that had dawned within her. "That's the journey of every soul, Aria. The search for purpose, for meaning, for love—it all comes back to the same thing. You're searching for yourself. For the truth of who you are."

Aria stared into the reflection, watching as the image shifted again. Now, it showed her in yet another life, a life where she had been filled with ambition and drive, chasing success and recognition. She had believed, in that life, that her worth was tied to her accomplishments—that if she could just achieve enough, she would finally find the validation she sought.

But the reflection showed her something different. It showed her the emptiness that had followed each achievement, the hollow feeling that came from chasing external validation. She had achieved much in that life, but the search for purpose had remained unfulfilled.

"I was looking in the wrong places," Aria said, her voice heavy with understanding. "I thought purpose was something I had to find in the world, something I had to achieve. But it was never out there. It was always within me."

Her Self pulsed with warmth, the light of its form growing brighter. "Yes, Aria. That's the truth. The purpose you've been searching for isn't something you have to achieve. It's something you *are*. It's who you've always been."

Aria took a deep breath, her eyes still locked on the shifting reflections. The images before her showed her many lives, many versions of herself—each one different, but each one carrying the same search, the same desire for meaning. In every life, she had been seeking something outside herself, but the answer had always been within.

"The Other was never separate from me," she said, her voice soft but filled with certainty. "Their search is my search. Their purpose is my purpose."

Her Self smiled, the glow of its presence wrapping around her like a comforting embrace. "Exactly. And now you understand. The reflection of the Other was meant to show you that you are not alone in your search. Every soul, every being, is part of the same journey. And that journey always leads back to the Self."

Aria's heart swelled with a sense of peace she hadn't known before. She had spent so many lifetimes searching, so many lives chasing after purpose, meaning, and validation. But now, in this moment, she understood that the search had never been about finding something external. It had always been about remembering who she truly was.

"Purpose isn't something to find," Aria said quietly, her voice filled with reverence. "It's something to remember."

Her Self shimmered, its light radiating with joy. "Yes. The Re-Genesis isn't about creating something new. It's about remembering what has always been true. You are already whole. You are already enough. And so is the Other. So is every soul."

Aria stared into the cosmic mirror one last time, watching as the reflections shifted and merged, showing her the interconnectedness of all life. Every soul, every journey, every experience was woven together, part of the same cosmic tapestry. The search for purpose was universal, and yet, it always led back to the same place—back to the Self.

She turned to her Self, her heart full of love, understanding, and a deep sense of peace. "I see it now. We are all connected. We are all reflections of each other, searching for the same truth."

Her Self smiled, its form glowing with warmth and love. "And now that you've seen the reflection, you are ready to help others see it too."

Aria nodded, her soul filled with quiet certainty. She was ready. The Re-Genesis wasn't just about her own awakening—it was about helping others remember the truth of who they were. It was about guiding them to see their own reflection in the cosmic mirror, to understand that they were already whole, already enough.

The reflections around her shimmered, the cosmic mirror rippling as it dissolved into the golden light. Aria stood in the stillness, her heart open, her mind clear.

She was ready to be the reflection of light for others.

And in doing so, she would help them remember that they, too, were the light they had been searching for all along.

8

The Awakening

As the cosmic mirror dissolved into golden light, Aria stood alone in the quiet, vast expanse. The reflections had faded, but their truths remained with her, settled deep within her heart. She had seen it now—truly seen it. The connection between herself and the Other, between herself and all souls, was undeniable. They were not separate, not truly. They were all part of the same journey, the same dance, all searching for the same truth.

The light around her began to shift once more, and Aria felt herself being drawn into a new vision. This time, there was no city, no bench, no bustling crowds. Instead, she found herself in a tranquil garden, filled with soft light and the scent of blooming flowers. The air was calm, filled with the quiet hum of life. Birds sang in the distance, and a gentle breeze rustled the leaves of the trees around her.

And there, in the center of the garden, sat the Other.

They were no longer surrounded by chaos, no longer searching frantically for something they couldn't name. Instead, they sat in stillness, their eyes closed, their breath slow and steady. There was a calmness about them now, a sense of peace that hadn't been there before.

Aria hovered nearby, watching with quiet awe. The Other was awakening. She could feel it—their energy had shifted, their presence more grounded, more centered. There was no more rushing, no more desperation. They had found stillness, and in that stillness, they had begun to remember.

"They're starting to see," Aria whispered, her heart swelling with quiet pride.

Her Self appeared beside her, once again as a glowing figure of light. "Yes," it said softly, its voice filled with warmth. "The search for purpose is over. They are beginning to awaken to the truth."

Aria watched as the Other opened their eyes, their gaze soft and unfocused, as though they were seeing the world through new eyes. They didn't move right away. Instead, they sat in the stillness, breathing in the quiet peace of the garden around them.

"They're realizing," Aria said, her voice barely above a whisper. "They're realizing that they don't need to search anymore."

Her Self nodded. "The awakening isn't a moment of grand revelation, Aria. It's a quiet remembering. It's the realization that the purpose they were searching for was never out there—it was always within."

Aria felt a deep sense of connection to the Other as she watched them sit in the garden, their eyes slowly scanning the beauty around them. The flowers, the trees, the soft light—all of it seemed to glow with a new energy, as if the world itself was waking up alongside them.

"They're seeing the world differently," Aria said softly, a smile tugging at her lips. "It's like... everything is brighter, more alive."

Her Self's light pulsed gently. "That's the gift of awakening. When you remember who you are, when you stop searching for purpose outside of yourself, the world around you becomes clearer. You begin to see the beauty that was always there, hidden beneath the distractions and the noise."

Aria nodded, her heart full. She had felt this before, in her own moments of awakening—those quiet moments when everything seemed to click into place, when the world suddenly made sense in a way it hadn't before. It wasn't about achieving something or reaching some grand goal. It was about remembering. About seeing the truth that had always been there.

"The Other is starting to understand that they don't need to be anything more than who they are," Aria said, her voice filled with quiet certainty. "They're letting go of the need to prove themselves, to find meaning in accomplishments."

Her Self smiled, the light around it shimmering with approval. "Yes. And that is the true awakening. It's not about becoming something new—it's about recognizing that you've always been enough. The search for purpose is over because purpose was never something to be found. It was always part of who they are."

Aria's gaze softened as she watched the Other stand from their seat in the garden, their movements slow and deliberate. There was no rush, no sense of urgency. They moved with a quiet grace, their presence calm and centered. They had found peace, not because they had achieved something or discovered a hidden truth, but because they had let go of the need to search.

"They're at peace with themselves," Aria said, her heart swelling with love. "They've stopped trying to be more, to do more."

Her Self's voice was soft, filled with affection. "That's the gift of awakening. When you realize that you are enough, just as you are, the need for striving falls away. You begin to move through life with a sense of ease, a sense of grace. You stop fighting the flow, and instead, you allow yourself to be carried by it."

Aria watched as the Other walked slowly through the garden, their hands brushing gently against the flowers as they passed. There was a lightness to their steps now, a sense of joy that came not from external achievement, but from an internal knowing. They were no longer searching for purpose. They were living it.

"They're no longer lost," Aria whispered, her voice filled with quiet awe. "They've found themselves."

Her Self nodded, its light glowing brighter with each word. "Yes. And now that they've awakened to their own truth, they will begin to share that truth with others. That's the final step of the journey, Aria. Once you've remembered who you are, once you've found your own light, you are called to share that light with the world."

Aria's heart swelled with understanding. She had seen this in her own journey—the way her awakening had led her to help others, to guide them toward their own truth. And now, the Other was beginning to walk the same path. They had awakened to their own light, and soon, they would share that light with the world around them.

"They'll help others see the truth," Aria said softly, a smile touching her lips. "They'll help others remember who they are."

Her Self's voice was warm, filled with quiet joy. "Yes. That is the gift of awakening. It's not just for you. It's for everyone. When one person awakens, they become a beacon of light, a guide for others who are still searching in the dark. The Other will become a guide, just as you have been a guide."

Aria watched as the Other continued to walk through the garden, their face turned up toward the soft light of the sun. There was a peace in their expression, a quiet joy that radiated from within. They had found their purpose, not in some grand achievement or external validation, but in the simple act of being. They had remembered the truth of who they were, and in doing so, they had awakened to a deeper understanding of life.

"They'll continue to grow," Aria said softly, her voice filled with love. "They'll continue to learn, to evolve, but now they'll do it with the knowledge that they are already enough."

Her Self smiled, its light pulsing gently in the golden air. "Yes. And that is the beauty of awakening. It's not an endpoint. It's the beginning of a new journey. A journey of living with purpose, of sharing light, of helping others find their way."

Aria's heart swelled with joy as she watched the Other walk through the garden, their presence a reflection of peace, of love, of purpose. They had found their way, and now, they would help others do the same.

"The Re-Genesis is beginning," Aria said quietly, her voice filled with quiet conviction. "And it starts with each person remembering their own light."

Her Self's light shimmered with approval, its voice soft and filled with love. "Yes. And soon, the world will begin to awaken. One soul at a time, the light will spread, and humanity will remember the truth of who they are."

Aria smiled, her heart full of hope, of love, of certainty. The awakening had begun. The Re-Genesis was unfolding, not through grand acts of power, but through the quiet, gentle remembering of each soul's light.

And Aria knew that she would be there, guiding others, helping them remember, helping them awaken to the truth that had always been within them.

Because the light was not something to be found.

It was something to be remembered.

9

You Are the Other

As the light of the garden faded, Aria found herself in a new space—one that felt different from all the others she had visited before. This place was vast, but not in the boundless, cosmic sense she had experienced in the infinite realms. It felt intimate, like standing at the edge of a deep, personal truth, one she hadn't yet fully grasped.

Around her, there was a stillness. The air was thick with possibility, as though something profound was waiting just out of reach. Aria knew that whatever this space held, it was meant to reveal the final piece of her understanding. She had witnessed the Other's awakening, watched them remember their own truth. But there was something more—something she needed to see for herself.

Her Self appeared beside her, this time in a form that felt more familiar, more grounded. It was less ethereal now, its glow softer, more like a gentle presence than a cosmic guide.

"You've come far, Aria," her Self said, its voice calm, steady. "You've seen the journey of the Other, you've seen the awakening. But there's one more truth you need to understand."

Aria nodded, her heart filled with a quiet anticipation. She had felt this truth approaching, sensed it in the way the Other's life had mirrored her own. There had been moments, flickers of understanding, but now, standing in this still, quiet space, she knew that the time had come to face it fully.

Her Self gestured toward the empty space before them, and slowly, a reflection began to form. At first, it was hazy, like looking through a fogged mirror. But as the image sharpened, Aria saw something she hadn't expected.

It wasn't the Other standing in the reflection.

It was *her*.

Aria's breath caught in her throat as she stared at her own reflection, watching as her face took shape in the shimmering surface. She looked just as she had in this current life—her familiar features, her own eyes staring back at her. But there was something more in this reflection, something that went beyond just physical appearance.

"I'm... the Other," Aria whispered, her voice barely audible.

Her Self stood beside her, its presence warm and reassuring. "Yes. You've always been the Other, Aria. The life you've been witnessing, the search for purpose, the struggle, the awakening—it's all been a reflection of your own journey."

Aria's mind spun as she stared at her reflection, the weight of her Self's words settling over her. She had spent so much time watching the Other, feeling their struggle, their longing for meaning, their journey toward awakening. And now, she realized that every step of their path had been her own.

"You were never separate from them," her Self continued, its voice gentle but firm. "The Other was always a reflection of you. Their search for purpose, their awakening, their remembering—it was all your story."

Aria took a deep breath, her heart pounding in her chest as the truth washed over her. She had seen it in glimpses, felt it in the way her connection to the Other had deepened with each passing moment. But now, she understood it fully. The Other was not just another soul on their own journey. They were *her*. Their life, their experiences, their struggles—they were her own, reflected back to her through the lens of another.

"I've been witnessing myself," Aria said softly, her voice trembling with the weight of the realization. "All this time... it was me."

Her Self nodded, its light pulsing gently beside her. "Yes. And this is the final truth you needed to understand. The Re-Genesis isn't just about helping others awaken—it's about awakening to the fact that you are not separate from them. You are the Other, and the Other is you. There is no separation."

Aria's heart swelled with a mixture of awe and humility. She had spent so many lifetimes searching for purpose, for meaning, for connection. She had seen the Other's journey as something outside of herself, something she was meant to guide and witness. But now, she understood that their journey had been her own all along.

"Their struggles were my struggles," Aria whispered, her voice filled with quiet reverence. "Their doubts, their fears... they were all mine."

Her Self's voice was soft, filled with compassion. "Yes. You've been walking the same path. And now you see the truth—there is no 'Other.' There is only you. And when you help others awaken, you are helping yourself awaken, too."

Aria stood in silence, her mind reeling with the magnitude of what she had just uncovered. The search for purpose, the journey toward awakening—it had never been about guiding someone else. It had always been about her. Every life she had lived, every person she had encountered, every soul she had helped—it had all been part of the same cosmic dance, the same reflection of herself.

"The Re-Genesis isn't just a cosmic restart for the world," Aria said slowly, her eyes still locked on her reflection. "It's a rebirth of *me*."

Her Self smiled, the warmth of its presence wrapping around her like a comforting embrace. "Yes. The Re-Genesis is a remembering, not just for humanity, but for you. It's the moment when you realize that the journey isn't about helping others find their light. It's about realizing that their light is your light. You are not separate from them. You are One."

Aria's heart swelled with love, with understanding, with a deep sense of unity. She had spent so many lifetimes searching for connection, for a sense of belonging. And now, in this quiet moment, she realized that she had always belonged. She had always been connected. There was no separation between herself and the souls she had encountered. They were all reflections of the same light, the same source.

"I've been helping myself all along," Aria said softly, her voice filled with wonder. "Every soul I've guided, every person I've helped awaken—it was all part of my own awakening."

Her Self nodded, its form glowing brighter with each word. "Yes. And now you understand. The Re-Genesis isn't just a new beginning for the world—it's a new beginning for you. You've remembered the truth of who you are. You've remembered that you are the light you've been searching for."

Aria smiled, her heart full of love, of peace, of clarity. She no longer felt the weight of her search for purpose, no longer felt the need to strive for something outside of herself. She had found the truth she had been seeking all along. The light she had been searching for was her own.

"There is no Other," Aria whispered, her eyes soft as she gazed at her reflection. "There is only me."

Her Self's light pulsed one last time, a gentle affirmation of the truth Aria had uncovered. "And now that you've remembered, you are free. Free to live with purpose, free to share your light, free to help others remember their own."

Aria took a deep breath, her heart swelling with gratitude. She had come so far, traveled through so many lifetimes, all in search of the same truth. And now, standing in this quiet, sacred space, she knew that her journey was not just about awakening others—it was about awakening herself. And in doing so, she would help others see that they, too, were not separate. They, too, were part of the same light.

"I'm ready," Aria said softly, her voice filled with quiet certainty. "I'm ready to share my light, to help others see the truth in themselves."

Her Self smiled, its form beginning to dissolve into the golden light. "You are the light, Aria. And now, you are free to shine."

As her Self faded into the golden glow, Aria stood alone in the vast, shimmering space. But she didn't feel alone. She felt connected, whole, complete. She had found her truth, her purpose, her light.

And as the final reflections dissolved around her, Aria knew that the Re-Genesis had already begun.

It wasn't something that would happen in the future.

It was happening now, in this moment, in her.

Because the light she had been searching for wasn't something outside of herself.

It was *her*.

And now, she was ready to share that light with the world.

Part Four

THE RE-GENESIS

10

Beginning Again

The golden light around Aria pulsed softly, like the first breath of a newborn dawn. Everything felt new, as though the entire universe had shifted subtly, but profoundly, and the weight of lifetimes had lifted from her shoulders. She stood in a familiar yet transformed space—an ethereal bridge between the infinite and the tangible world she was preparing to return to.

This was the moment of Re-Genesis.

But it didn't feel like an ending. It felt like the beginning of something far greater, something that had always been there, waiting for her to see it. Aria had journeyed through lifetimes, learning, forgetting, and remembering again. She had searched for her purpose, tried to find herself in others, and now she had come full circle.

The Other had been her all along. The struggles she had witnessed, the desire for meaning, the quiet yearning for connection—it was all her own. And now, the Re-Genesis was not only a rebirth for the world, but a rebirth for her as well.

Her Self appeared beside her, glowing softly, a familiar presence that no longer felt separate from her, but rather an extension of who she truly was.

"You're ready, Aria," her Self said, its voice filled with quiet pride. "You've remembered the truth, and now it's time to begin again. But this time, you won't be searching for yourself. You'll be living as yourself, fully and without hesitation."

Aria smiled, feeling the warmth of those words settle into her heart. She was no longer the seeker, no longer chasing after some elusive purpose. She had found it—found herself. And now, she was ready to live with that knowledge, to embody the light she had always carried within her.

"The Re-Genesis isn't just a new beginning for the world," Aria said softly, her voice steady. "It's a new beginning for me. I'm starting over, but this time, I know who I am."

Her Self's light shimmered in agreement. "Yes. And that's the key to the Re-Genesis, Aria. It's not about creating something entirely new—it's about returning to the truth that has always been within you. You're not becoming something different. You're remembering who you've always been."

Aria took a deep breath, feeling the weight of those words sink in. She had spent so long believing that purpose was something she had to find, something she had to become. But now she knew that it wasn't about striving, or achieving, or chasing after something outside of herself. It was about embracing who she already was—living fully in her truth, and in doing so, helping others remember theirs.

"What happens now?" Aria asked, her gaze drifting toward the horizon, where the light of the world she was returning to shimmered just out of reach.

Her Self smiled softly. "Now, you begin again. But this time, you'll walk with purpose, not because you're searching for it, but because you are it. You'll live as a reminder to those who are still searching—showing them through your light that they, too, can remember who they are."

Aria's heart swelled with love, with hope, with quiet determination. The Re-Genesis wasn't just for her—it was for everyone. It was a cosmic shift, a moment of awakening, when humanity would begin to remember the truth of who they were. But that awakening wouldn't come through force or grand gestures. It would come through quiet moments of connection, through the gentle unfolding of light in each person's heart.

She turned to her Self, her eyes filled with a quiet certainty. "I'm ready."

Her Self nodded, the light around it pulsing with approval. "I know you are. And remember, Aria—this journey isn't about perfection. It's about love. The love you give, the love you receive, and the love you *are*. That's the heart of the Re-Genesis."

Aria smiled, her heart full of peace. She had learned so much, but the greatest lesson had been the simplest: love was the only truth that mattered. It was the foundation of everything—the force that connected all beings, the light that guided every soul. And now, she would carry that love with her, sharing it with the world as she began her new life.

The golden light around her began to shift, and Aria felt the gentle pull of the world she was returning to. It was time. Time to step back into the flow of life, to live fully, to embody the light she had always carried within her.

Her Self lingered beside her for a moment longer, its presence a comforting reminder that she was never truly alone.

"Remember, Aria," her Self said softly, "you are the light you've been searching for. And now, it's time to share that light with the world."

Aria nodded, her heart filled with love, with purpose, with the quiet certainty that she was exactly where she needed to be. She had been through so many lifetimes, so many lessons, but now, she was ready to live with full awareness of who she truly was.

With one final breath, Aria stepped forward, into the shimmering light of the world below. The golden glow wrapped around her like a warm embrace, pulling her gently into the flow of life once more.

But this time, it was different.

This time, she wasn't returning as a seeker, lost in the search for purpose or meaning. She was returning as herself—whole, complete, and fully awake to the truth that had always been within her.

As the light of the world enveloped her, Aria felt the gentle hum of life around her, the pulse of existence that connected every soul, every breath, every moment. She was part of it, and yet, she was also the light that illuminated it.

The Re-Genesis had begun.

Not as a single moment of transformation, but as a quiet, continuous unfolding—a remembering of the truth that had always been there.

And as Aria stepped fully into her new beginning, she knew, with every fiber of her being, that this was where she was meant to be.

Not searching.

Not striving.

But simply *being*.

Living her truth.

Sharing her light.

Beginning again, with love.

Always with love.

11

The Seed of Light

The world around Aria shimmered as she stepped fully into her new beginning. The golden light of the Re-Genesis had wrapped her in its warmth, and now, as it faded, she found herself in a quiet, peaceful place. The air was fresh, carrying the scent of earth and life, and the sky above was painted with soft hues of dawn. It felt like the very first morning of a new world—a world reborn, yet familiar.

Aria stood in a vast field, the ground beneath her soft and fertile, as if waiting for something to take root. All around her, the earth hummed with potential, with the quiet promise of new life. The Re-Genesis had begun, not just in her but in the world itself. It was a subtle shift, a gentle awakening that had already started to ripple through the fabric of existence.

She could feel it in the air, in the soil beneath her feet—a sense that everything was connected, everything was growing. The world was coming alive in a way that it hadn't before, as if the light she carried within her had awakened something deep within the earth itself.

Aria knelt down, her fingers brushing the ground. It was warm to the touch, alive with energy. She closed her eyes, feeling the pulse of life beneath her, the quiet rhythm of the universe that had always been there, waiting for this moment.

"This is where it begins," her Self's voice whispered softly, its presence close but invisible. "This is where you plant the seed of light."

Aria opened her eyes, her gaze soft as she looked down at the earth before her. She knew what her Self meant. This wasn't about planting a physical seed—this was about planting the light she carried within her, allowing it to take root in the world, to grow and spread, touching every soul it encountered.

She had learned so much on her journey, but now it was time to share that knowledge, to offer her light to the world. The Re-Genesis wasn't just her own awakening—it was a call to help others awaken as well. And the seed of light she was about to plant would be the first step in that process.

Aria reached into the depths of her heart, feeling the warmth of the light she had carried for so long. It was a quiet, gentle light, but it was powerful. It had always been there, waiting for the moment when she was ready to share it. And now, that moment had come.

She cupped her hands together, and as she did, a small, glowing seed appeared in her palms. It pulsed softly with the same golden light that had surrounded her in the infinite space. This was her light—the essence of who she was, the truth she had remembered.

With a deep breath, Aria pressed the seed into the earth, her hands gently covering it with soil. As she did, she whispered softly, her voice filled with love and intention.

"Let this light grow," she said, her words a quiet prayer to the universe. "Let it take root in the hearts of those who are ready. Let it spread, not through force, but through love. Let it remind them of who they are."

The earth beneath her hands seemed to hum in response, a gentle affirmation of the truth she had planted. Aria sat back, her heart full, her eyes soft as she watched the soil where the seed had been buried. It was small, almost invisible now, but she knew that it would grow. It would spread, not just in the physical world, but in the hearts and minds of those who needed it most.

"This is how the Re-Genesis begins," her Self said softly, its presence a warm glow around her. "Not with grand gestures or dramatic changes, but with quiet acts of love. Each seed you plant, each light you share, will ripple outwards, touching others, awakening them to the truth of who they are."

Aria smiled, her heart light. She understood now that her role wasn't to change the world all at once. It was to plant seeds, to offer her light to those who were ready, and to trust that, in time, those seeds would grow. The Re-Genesis wasn't about forcing a transformation—it was about nurturing it, allowing it to unfold naturally, in its own time.

"They'll find their way," Aria said softly, her gaze still fixed on the soil where the seed lay buried. "Just like I did."

Her Self's voice was warm with approval. "Yes. And you'll be there to guide them, not by leading them, but by walking beside them. The light you've planted will grow, but it will do so because they choose to nurture it themselves. That's the beauty of the Re-Genesis—it's not something that happens to them. It's something they create within themselves."

Aria nodded, feeling the truth of those words resonate deep within her. She had been guided by her own Self, by the quiet whispers of truth that had always been there, waiting for her to listen. And now, she would become that quiet whisper for others, offering her light, her love, and trusting that they, too, would remember who they were.

She stood, her hands still warm from the act of planting, and looked out across the field. It stretched endlessly before her, a vast expanse of untapped potential. There was so much work to be done, so many souls still searching for their own light. But Aria didn't feel overwhelmed. She felt ready. Ready to walk this path, to share her light, to help others plant their own seeds of truth.

"You've planted the first seed," her Self said, its voice filled with quiet joy. "And now, you'll plant more, not just here, but in every life you touch, in every soul you meet."

Aria smiled, her heart full of love. She could feel the light within her growing, expanding, reaching out into the world around her. This was her purpose—not to change the world herself, but to inspire others to do it. To help them remember the light they carried, the truth they had always known.

"I'll keep planting," Aria said softly, her voice steady with quiet determination. "I'll keep sharing my light, and I'll trust that it will grow."

Her Self shimmered beside her, its presence a quiet confirmation of the path ahead. "That's all you need to do, Aria. The light you plant will grow because love always grows. It cannot be contained. It cannot be forced. It simply is."

Aria took a deep breath, feeling the weight of those words settle into her bones. The Re-Genesis was not a single moment. It was a process, a journey that would unfold over time, through small acts of love, through seeds of light planted in the hearts of those who were ready to awaken.

She looked out across the field once more, her heart swelling with love for the world, for humanity, for the infinite potential that lay before her.

"I'm ready," Aria whispered, her voice filled with quiet certainty. "I'm ready to help them remember."

And with that, she began to walk, her steps light, her heart full, her path clear.

The Re-Genesis had begun.

And Aria was planting the seeds that would help it grow.

12

The Eternal Return

Aria walked across the field, her steps light, her heart full of quiet purpose. The golden light of the Re-Genesis pulsed softly around her, like a gentle heartbeat in tune with the earth beneath her feet. She had planted the first seed of light, knowing that it would grow, that it would spread—not through grand acts, but through love. Her journey was far from over, but it had taken on a new meaning, a new depth. The search was no longer about finding herself—it was about sharing the light she had always carried within her.

The field stretched out endlessly before her, but Aria didn't feel overwhelmed by its vastness. She felt at peace, knowing that each step she took, each soul she touched, would plant another seed of light. And in time, those seeds would take root, just as hers had.

As she walked, her Self appeared beside her once more, glowing softly in the golden light. There was no need for words between them—Aria already understood the path she was on, and her Self was there to walk it with her, as it always had been.

"You're ready for what comes next," her Self said gently, breaking the silence, its voice warm with love. "You've planted the seed, and now the world will grow. But the Re-Genesis is more than just planting light—it's about the eternal return."

Aria looked at her Self, her brow furrowed slightly in thought. "The eternal return?"

Her Self nodded, its form shimmering softly in the golden air. "The Re-Genesis is not a single event, Aria. It's a cycle. A continual process of remembering, of awakening, of returning to the truth over and over again. Each time you plant a seed of light, you begin the cycle again, not just for others, but for yourself."

Aria thought about the countless lives she had lived, the journeys she had taken, the lessons she had learned and forgotten and learned again. It was all part of the same cycle, the same process of returning to the truth. She had sought the light in so many ways, but each time, she had eventually found herself back at the same place—back at the source, back to love.

"The eternal return," Aria said softly, understanding dawning within her. "We keep coming back to the same truth, don't we? Over and over, until we finally remember it fully."

Her Self smiled, its light pulsing in gentle approval. "Yes. That's the heart of the Re-Genesis. It's not about achieving perfection or reaching some final destination. It's about the journey itself—the continual process of awakening, of returning to love, of remembering who we are."

Aria nodded, feeling the weight of those words settle into her heart. The journey wasn't linear. It wasn't about climbing a mountain and reaching the top. It was a spiral, a dance of returning to the same truth from new perspectives, with new understanding, each time deepening the connection to the light within.

She had spent lifetimes searching for that truth, seeking it in the world around her, only to realize that it had always been within her. And now, she would return again, not as a seeker, but as a guide. She would help others remember, help them awaken to their own light, just as she had.

"The Re-Genesis is eternal," Aria said quietly, her voice filled with quiet reverence. "We return to it again and again, each time deeper, each time with more love."

Her Self's voice was warm, full of love and understanding. "Yes. And each time you return, you carry more light with you. Each time you awaken, you help others do the same. The Re-Genesis is not an end—it is a continual unfolding of light, a return to the beginning, again and again."

Aria looked out across the field, her heart swelling with love for the journey she had taken, for the light she had found within herself. She knew now that the journey would never truly end. She would keep returning, keep planting seeds of light, keep helping others awaken to the truth of who they were. And in doing so, she would continue to grow, continue to return to the source of her own light.

"I'll keep coming back," Aria said softly, her voice filled with quiet determination. "I'll keep returning, keep sharing my light, until everyone remembers."

Her Self smiled, its presence warm and comforting beside her. "And in each return, you'll find new ways to shine, new ways to guide, new ways to love. That is the gift of the eternal return—it is never the same, but it is always true."

Aria took a deep breath, her heart full of gratitude for the journey she had taken, and for the journey that still lay ahead. The Re-Genesis was not just a new beginning for the world—it was a new beginning for her, over and over again, with each return, with each step.

And now, as she walked through the field, her steps light and sure, she knew that she was exactly where she needed to be. The world around her shimmered with potential, with the quiet promise of growth, of awakening, of love. Each seed she planted, each light she shared, would continue the cycle, would continue the eternal return.

"I'll keep planting," Aria whispered, her voice soft but filled with certainty. "I'll keep sharing my light, and I'll keep returning to love."

Her Self shimmered beside her, its presence a quiet affirmation of the path she had chosen. "And each time you return, you'll carry more light with you, Aria. The Re-Genesis is not just a beginning—it's a reminder that love is always present, always waiting to be remembered."

Aria smiled, her heart light and full of peace. She understood now that the journey wasn't about reaching a final destination. It was about returning to the truth, again and again, deepening her connection to the light within her, and sharing that light with the world.

The field stretched endlessly before her, but Aria didn't feel daunted by its vastness. She felt ready, her heart full of love, her steps sure. She would walk this path, not just once, but over and over again, each time returning with more light, more love, more understanding.

The Re-Genesis was eternal.

And so was she.

With one last look at the endless field before her, Aria took a deep breath and began to walk, her heart full of purpose, her steps light with love.

Because the Re-Genesis wasn't something that happened once.

It was the eternal return.

A return to love.

A return to light.

A return to the truth that had always been within her.

And with each step, she would carry that light forward, planting seeds, sharing love, and trusting that the journey would continue.

Because the journey never ended.

It only began again.

With love.

Always with love.

Epilogue

The Light in You

The world Aria had returned to was no longer the same, though it looked unchanged on the surface. The quiet hum of life continued—people moved through their routines, the sun rose and set, and the seasons turned. Yet, beneath it all, something deeper had shifted, something that would unfold over time. The Re-Genesis had begun, not with a grand explosion of light or a sweeping transformation, but with quiet, personal awakenings—small seeds of truth planted in the hearts of those ready to remember.

And now, it is your turn.

You, the one holding this story, the one reading these words. You are not separate from the journey. Aria's path, her search for meaning, her awakening to the light within—it mirrors your own. Her story is not just a tale of one soul's discovery. It is a reflection of the truth that lives within *you*.

There is a light inside you, a light that has always been there. Perhaps you've felt it before, in fleeting moments of clarity, in the quiet space between thoughts, in the stillness of the night when the noise of the world fades and you are left with only yourself. Or perhaps it feels distant, like a faint memory of something you've forgotten, something you long to return to.

But whether you are aware of it or not, that light is there. It is part of you, woven into the very fabric of your being. And just as Aria discovered, it is not something you need to search for in the world outside of you. It is not something to be earned or achieved. It is simply who you are.

The Re-Genesis is not just a story. It is a call to remember. A call to awaken to the light that you already carry within you.

As you've walked with Aria through her journey, you may have seen glimpses of your own reflection in her struggles, her doubts, her moments of clarity. You may have felt the stirring of something familiar in her search for purpose, in her desire to make sense of the world. And now, you stand at the threshold of your own Re-Genesis, your own moment of remembering.

This is your time. This is your moment to awaken to the truth of who you are. To realize that you, too, carry the seed of light within you. And just like Aria, you are being called to plant that seed, to let it take root and grow, not only within yourself but in the world around you.

The Re-Genesis is not something that happens to the world. It is something that happens *through* each of us. It happens when we choose to live with love, with purpose, with the quiet understanding that we are already enough. That we are already whole.

And so, I ask you: What will you do with the light you carry? How will you plant your seed of truth in the world? How will you let your light shine, not for the sake of recognition or achievement, but simply because it is who you are?

This is not a challenge. It is an invitation. An invitation to return to the truth you've always known, the truth that lives within your heart.

You are the light.

You are the Re-Genesis.

The journey is yours now, and the light is already within you. You don't need to search for it. You don't need to strive for it. All you need to do is remember.

And once you remember, you will know what to do.

You will know how to live with purpose, how to love without condition, how to plant seeds of light in the hearts of others. You will know that the journey is not about finding something outside of yourself, but about awakening to the truth that has always been within you.

So, take a moment.

Breathe.

Feel the quiet hum of life surrounding you, the subtle energy flowing beneath your feet, the connection between all things. In this stillness, sense the light within you—the gentle, unwavering glow that has always been a part of you.

Now, know this:

You are not separate from Aria's journey. Her story is also yours. The light you've read about, the awakening you've witnessed, is a reflection of the same light and truth within you. You are part of this Re-Genesis. You are part of the same endless cycle of awakening, remembering, and returning to love.

The Re-Genesis is not something happening *out there*—it's happening within *you*. Right now.

And now, it's your turn to carry that light forward.

You don't need to search for it. You don't need to strive to become something more. All you need to do is *remember* who you are. The light is already there, waiting to be shared, waiting to guide others, waiting to ripple out and touch the world.

So, go ahead.

Plant your own seed of light.

Shine brightly, not because you must prove yourself, but because it is your nature to shine. And through your light, others will begin to see their own.

Remember, you are enough. You are already whole. You carry the light that the world needs, and it is waiting for you to share it.

This journey, this Re-Genesis, is now yours.

So take the next step.

In love.

Always in love.